THIS BOOK BELONGS TO

....

Editor Jane O'Shea
Art editor Alison Fenton
Assisted by Hazel Bennington
and Alison Barclay
Production Jill Macey

First published in 1992 by
Conran Octopus Limited
37 Shelton Street, London WC2H 9HN

© text 1992 Frank Muir
© illustrations 1992 Graham Philpot

ISBN 1 85029 416 X

Imagesetting by Cymbol, London
Colour reproduction by Reed Reprographics, Suffolk
Printed and bound in Singapore

FRANK MUIR

RETELLS

GOLDILOCKS AND THE THREE BEARS

THE EXCITING STORY OF A SMALL BEAR . . .
A MEDIUM-SIZED BEAR . . . AN ENORMOUS BEAR
. . . AND A YOUNG GIRL WITH PROBLEM HAIR

Illustrated by Graham Philpot

CONRAN OCTOPUS

ONCE UPON A TIME, about a hundred and fifty years ago as the crow flies, our exciting yet heart-warming story began.

It was the London of Queen Victoria. Cobbled streets, fog, the Artful Dodger brushing against gentlemen and stealing their silk handkerchiefs. Fagin, the master pickpocket, brushing against the Artful Dodger and stealing the hankies back again. Scrooge, the miser, counting the coins in his pocket on his birthday and wondering whether he should go party-mad and buy himself a glass of water.

The heroine of our story was a young girl called Wonkybonce, the only daughter of a rich manufacturer.

She was known as Wonkybonce because her bonce (an old word meaning head) was wonky (an old word meaning wonky): the girl had Problem Hair. Yards and yards of it. And it was not only a nasty colour – off-black with dun-coloured streaks – but it was wild and tangled.

Wonkybonce HATED her hair.
She hated it with a capital HAY.
   When she was tiny she had
longed for long golden
locks, silky and shining
in the sun but she
grew up with a mop
of hair as unkempt
as a carthorse's
ankle and the
disappointment
changed her
from a nice
child into a
little horror.

Wonkybonce grew up to be a wicked little girl and things came to a head when she was horrible to the boys and girls in her school, Mrs Thunderbag's Academy for Gentlefolk. She told them fibs.

She told them that sausages were pig's eggs. And they believed her.

She told them that mice grew up to be dogs. And dogs grew up to be horses. And horses grew up to be elephants. And they believed her.

So she told them that if they unscrewed their tummy-buttons their bottoms would fall off.

That did it. That night all the little boys and girls tried to unscrew their tummy-buttons. But their bottoms did not fall off and the boys and girls only made their tummy-buttons sore and they cried all night and told their parents in the morning what Wonky had said.

The parents, outraged at Wonky's fibs, marched on Mrs Thunderbag's Academy, waving umbrellas, and took their children away.

The Academy had to close and Mrs Thunderbag sued Wonky's father for ruining her. She claimed damages of three million pounds (£3,000,000), which was a lot of money in those days.

Wonky's father, an important businessman, whom Wonky hardly ever saw (and who could never remember her name when they *did* meet) was fat and mauve-faced. He was having breakfast when Wonky's mother read out the solicitor's letter telling him that he was being sued.

'What!' he bellowed angrily. 'WHAT!!'

Wonky's mother, a timid hungry lady, watched miserably as her husband helped himself to both the fried eggs.

'I told you to stop that daughter of yours telling fibs!' he bellowed. 'It's all *your* fault!' And he began to beat his dear wife about the ears with a cold fried egg.

Wonky's hungry mother took no notice. She was busily trying to catch bits of cold egg yolk in her mouth.

Wonky heard the noise down in the coal-cellar where she slept. She crept upstairs, opened the door of the dining-room and walked in.

Her father saw her and froze.

'Who the devil are you?' he bellowed. 'What are you doing in my house?'

'She's our *daughter*!' said Wonky's mother. 'Don't you recognise our darling little – er – what's-er-name?' And then to Wonky: 'I wish you'd do something about your awful hair, dear'.

'Now look here you, er – thingummybob!' shouted her father. 'I'm being sued for every penny I've got due to you and your fibs. Well, I'm not going to pay. I'm emigrating to Australia with my fortune and your dear mother here. We're going to make even more money over there, aren't we, my precious?'

'Could I have the other fried egg?' said Wonky's mother, reaching out with her fork.

'What is to become of me?' asked Wonky.

'I'll sell you to Mrs Quagmire, the grave-digger's wife, for five shillings; she's looking for a kitchen maid. You won't get paid but you'll get an hour off every other Christmas. Can I say fairer than that?'

Something snapped inside Wonkybonce's bonce.

'I won't go!' she cried. '*I won't! I WON'T!!*' and for the first time in her life she screamed.

It was a terrific scream which could be heard over eight miles away.

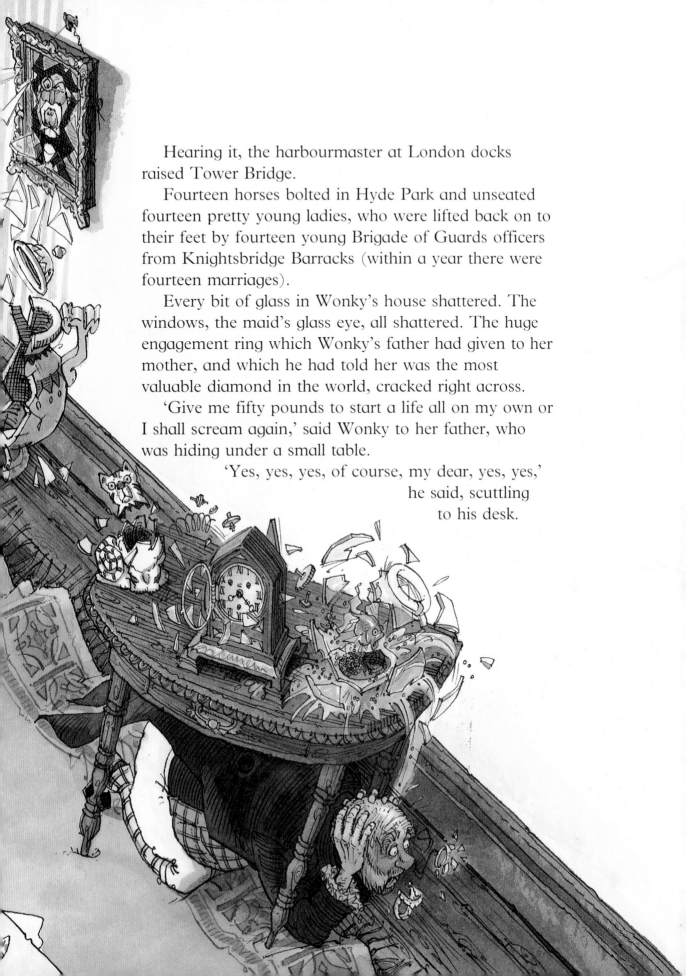

Hearing it, the harbourmaster at London docks raised Tower Bridge.

Fourteen horses bolted in Hyde Park and unseated fourteen pretty young ladies, who were lifted back on to their feet by fourteen young Brigade of Guards officers from Knightsbridge Barracks (within a year there were fourteen marriages).

Every bit of glass in Wonky's house shattered. The windows, the maid's glass eye, all shattered. The huge engagement ring which Wonky's father had given to her mother, and which he had told her was the most valuable diamond in the world, cracked right across.

'Give me fifty pounds to start a life all on my own or I shall scream again,' said Wonky to her father, who was hiding under a small table.

'Yes, yes, yes, of course, my dear, yes, yes,' he said, scuttling to his desk.

And so Wonkybonce left home, determined to make a nuisance of herself in the outside world.

She walked and walked and eventually found herself in a street of small houses.

A strange sight caught her attention. Over the rooftop of one of the houses a small, furry child rose into view, turned two and a half somersaults lazily in the air and then dropped out of sight.

Wonkybonce wandered over to find out what was going on. The front door was not locked so she walked in. On the kitchen table were three steaming bowls of porridge. She looked out of the window and saw that the furry child was not a furry child at all but a small bear. And the small bear was sitting on a see-saw with a medium-sized bear and a big bear.

The bears wanted to become circus acrobats. They rehearsed their act every morning while their porridge was cooling.

They were going to be called BORIS, DORIS AND HORACE - THE FLYING FLEABAGS.

The idea was that the small bear stood on the see-saw while at the other end the medium-sized bear balanced on the big bear's shoulders. There was a roll on the drums and the medium-sized bear jumped down onto the other end of the see-saw. The small bear shot up into the air, turned three somersaults and landed on the big bear's shoulders.

At least that was the idea. The trouble was that as soon as small Horace shot up he got air-sick and either turned two and a half somersaults and landed upside down on his father's head or missed him altogether and thudded onto the ground. They had never yet made the act work properly.

The three bears rehearsed pain-fully for a little while longer and then hurried in for their breakfast.

'SOMEBODY HAS BEEN EATING MY PORRIDGE!'

big Boris roared in his great rough, gruff voice.

'SOMEBODY HAS BEEN AT *MY* PORRIDGE, TOO!'

cried medium-sized Doris in her medium-sized voice.

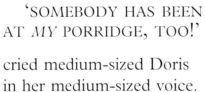

'Somebody has messed about with my porridge and gobbled it all up!'

howled small Horace in a tiny, aggrieved voice, holding up his empty bowl.

The big bear sat down in his easy chair to think things over but all the soft, comfortable cushions were missing and he sat down painfully on hard wood.

'SOMEBODY'S RUINED MY CHAIR!'

bellowed big Boris in his great rough, gruff voice.

'SOMEBODY'S TAKEN ALL THE CUSHIONS AWAY FROM MINE, TOO!'

complained medium-sized Doris, in her medium-sized voice.

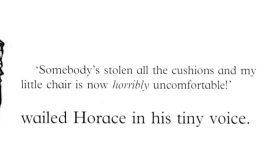

'Somebody's stolen all the cushions and my little chair is now *horribly* uncomfortable!'

wailed Horace in his tiny voice.

The big bear Boris was
now very angry and
determined to catch the
culprit. He rushed
upstairs to the bedroom,
followed by the others.

'LOOK!
SOMEBODY'S
TAKEN ALL MY
BED CLOTHES!'

thundered the big bear.

'SOMEBODY'S TAKEN
ALL *MY* BEDCLOTHES, TOO.'

wailed the medium-sized bear.

'Somebody's piled all
your pillows and bedclothes
on to my bed and climbed
under them, – *and here she is!!*'

cried the small bear.

And sure enough, there lay Wonkybonce, fast asleep, snug and warm and full of porridge, underneath all their cushions and bedclothes.

'WAKE UP! WHO ARE YOU?
WHAT ARE YOU DOING IN THAT BED?'

demanded the big bear. Wonkybonce woke up and glared fiercely at the big bear. 'It's *my* bed now,' she said firmly. 'I have decided to live here. I rather like porridge,' she added.

And so Wonkybonce took over their home. The bears were very kindly creatures but as the months went by, they became fed-up with her tantrums.

She made them bring her porridge in bed. She ate all their honey while they were out looking for work. And every evening she made each of them brush her horrible hair a hundred times to try to make it look better (it didn't).

'If you don't do what I want I'll scream!' she said.

'All right then, go ahead and scream!' said the big bear at last, angrily throwing her hairbrush out of the window.

So the naughty girl screamed again.

The gaslamp on the Eddystone lighthouse cracked and went out.

A seagull flying over the bears' house stopped flapping its wings and fell to the ground like a stone.

Mill hands in a town in Yorkshire thought it was their factory hooter blowing and went back to work.

From then on life grew worse for Boris, Doris and Horace. Wonkybonce bossed them about unmercifully and they could think of no way of getting rid of her.

17

Until one hot, sunny day in summer.

Wonkybonce was sunbathing on the see-saw. The three bears exchanged glances. The same thought occurred to them all. They crept upstairs. Horace's bedroom window was exactly above the see-saw.

Boris silently eased the window open. They climbed out. Clinging together, they balanced on the window-ledge for a moment then, at a nod from Boris – they jumped.

Half a ton of mixed bears plummeted down and with a mighty THUMP! landed on the other end of the see-saw.

Up in the air shot the sleeping Wonkybonce – up, up and away, in a gentle curve in the general direction of Hackney Marshes.

'Oh, what have we done!' cried Doris suddenly, paw to mouth. 'Perhaps we've killed her! Poor little thing, she wasn't really wicked, just unhappy - we must find her! Boris, *do* something!'

'She was flying towards Hackney Marshes,' cried Boris. 'It's not far on horseback.'

He ran to the paddock and brought out the ancient grey horse used to train circus bareback riders. He jumped into the saddle, Doris climbed up his back and balanced on his shoulders and Horace climbed up her back and balanced on *her* shoulders.

As soon as the horse started moving Horace got airsick, fell off and lay on the ground howling.

A few moments later Doris fell off into a flower-bed. Boris urged the old horse on but it was a good two hours before they reached Hackney Marshes.

There was no sign of poor Wonkybonce.

He asked everybody he met whether they had seen a plain little girl with lots of black hair but nobody had. Just as he was about to give up he met an old man with one tooth who was trying to eat an apple.

'About two hours ago it was,' said the old man. 'I saw something fall from the sky into Dibbledyke's Dye Works.'

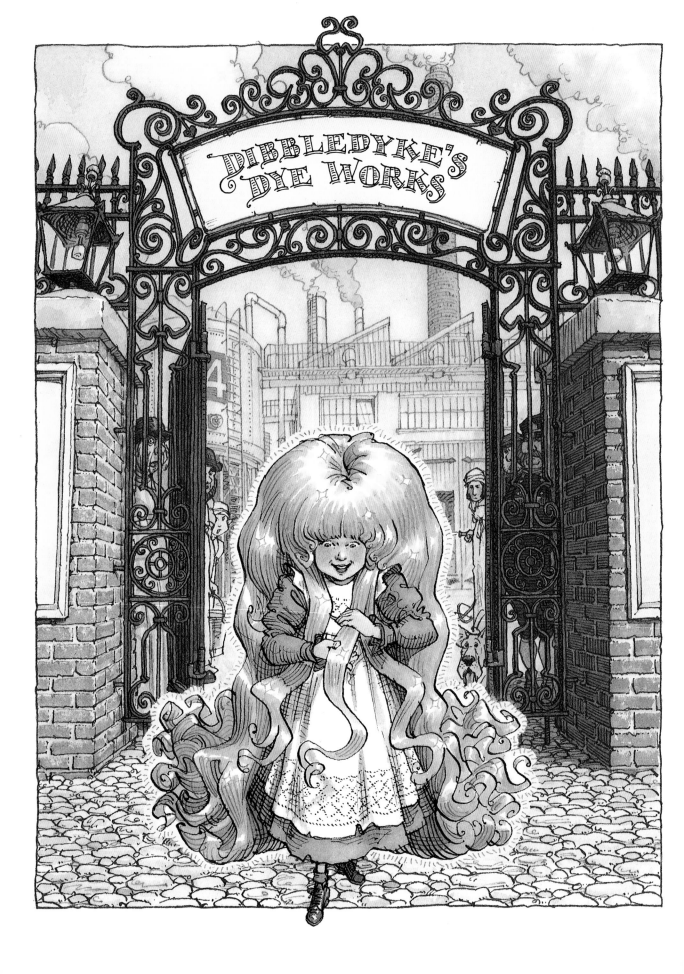

Boris urged the old horse towards the dye works. As he reached the gates a girl came out. She had long golden hair, silky and shining in the sun. She took up a handful of her lovely locks and looked at it, smiling happily to herself.

She *looked* like Wonkybonce. Except for the hair...

'No, you can't be Wonkybonce,' said Boris to the girl. 'She had awful hair. Yours is such a beautiful golden colour..!'

'I fell into No.4 Bleaching Vat,' said the girl.

'It *is* you!' cried Boris, leaning down and giving her a great bear hug. 'Wonderful! And I'll tell you what, little miss - nobody is ever going to call you Wonkybonce again! From now on your name is going to be –

GOLDILOCKS!'

'You've all been so kind to me,' said Goldilocks to the three bears when she and Boris got home. 'I promise I will never ever be nasty again. I enjoyed flying through the air so much that I would like to join your circus act!'

'Oh goody!' cried Horace. 'Now I can retire and never be airsick again!'

'Not quite,' said Goldilocks. 'You will be our manager and look after us because we are going to practise hard and be famous and perform all over the world. I'll make us brilliant costumes covered with sequins. But first we must have a new name for our act. The Flying Fleabags isn't *quite* what we want to call ourselves, is it?'

'I know!' cried Doris jumping up in excitement. 'How about -

GOLDILOCKS AND THE THREE BEARS!'

'Oh, perfect!' the others cried.